WET BRAIDS

Written by
Catherine Ayokosok

DEDICATION:

This piece is dedicated to my parents for teaching me to believe I could aim for the stars.

SUMMARY

Ngang is born in Cameroon to a loving family. She is the first daughter to be sent to boarding school. A teacher takes an interest in her, and she is able to immigrate to the United States with this woman where she grows up with a family in Virginia. Ngang is determined to make her family proud, and she successfully completes law school. She meets and falls in love with Kevin, who regularly cheats on her, but in her drive to succeed and create a family as she has been raised to believe is an essential part of a woman's life, she forgives him repeatedly. She loses her parents and then Ngang's Aunty, the woman who brought her to the States, has a stroke and a lengthy illness. In caring for and worrying about her Aunty, Ngang comes to realize what is really important in life. She reflects deeply on her beliefs, her own self-worth and her faith. She sees her experience reflected in other immigrants (Kevin, James and Fuale) who have struggled and she comes to realize the value of family, community and love. The story ends with some uncertainty as to whether she marries Kevin or not, but she has come to appreciate her life and her faith due to the experience of losing her parents and her Aunty.

CONTENTS

Loved by Everyone

It was the heart of the rainy season. The rain was pouring, the leaves were green and the harvest was plentiful. Every farmer was happy that year because the rains had been abundant and the crops were flourishing. The year before, the harvest suffered as the people could count the number of times it rained that year. With plenty of rain, there were fewer trips made by the children to the rivers to fetch water.

That August evening, the children were outside playing games in the rain in little groups. The boys were excited to play soccer in the mud while the girls were busy playing tag. No one wished for the rain to cease although it was getting darker. Finally ,darkness came, and parents called out for their children to come back home and rest. Reluctantly the children retired to their respective homes, looking forward to the next day to play again.

Mr.Zahn had five sons and a daughter. The younger three children of the Zahn family were usually outside playing like every other child in the neighborhood. They would play and forget that it was getting dark until their eldest brother came out looking for them. On this particular evening, Mr.Zahn had requested the children come home early because their mother was pregnant and he didn't want them coming home late to request a late supper.

"Children, get dry and hurry up for supper. We need to eat quickly so that I can get some rest," said Mrs. Zahn. She quickly arranged the table and had her daughter assist her. On the table was a bowl of water to wash hands, plates in the middle of the table and a big bowl of porridge cocoyams flavoured with dry fish. The whole family gathered around the table and Kosok, the eldest son, blessed the meal. During the meal, the children continued to talk to each other and play.

Mr.Zahn said, "Can you stop playing? You and your little brothers have to learn to eat your meal without playing. Don't you people get tired of playing? You just came from playing outside. Send me the bowl of yams, I need more." His long black arms stretched across the table to get the cocoyams as Akume walked towards her father and handed him the bowl.

"Thank you, Mama," Mr.Zahn smiled at his daughter

Mr. Zahn was a popular farmer and hunter who had worked hard to provide his family with one of the best standards of living in the community. Every planting season, he would invest in all his lands and at the end of harvest season, he would organize a feast with his neighbors celebrating his profits. Mr. Zahn would look up at the heavens and praise his ancestors for blessing him with the power to work.

"To the God of the heavens, thank you for blessing my hands and my family."

His annual feast was among the best in the town. The chief, Elders and influential people in the city were usual guests at Mr.Zahn's feast. At the feast, the village masquerades danced, people chanted and drank and everyone looked forward to the next harvest season.

At dawn the next morning, Mr.Zahn went out to the farms with his three eldest sons at dawn as they normally did. It had been many weeks of waiting for this baby and Mr. Zahn hoped that this morning was not the morning the baby would arrive. He left for the farms under the heavy rain with his sons.

Hours passed and while he was gone, Mrs.Zahn went into labour. She was in terrible pain and she kept groaning. Akume was at home with her two younger brothers and she ran, screaming for help as she ran to the neighbor's houses.

The women quickly rushed Mrs.Zahn to the hospital where she immediately delivered a beautiful baby girl born on the coast of

Cameroon on a rainy morning of August 4,1980. Mr.Zahn was sent for and when he came to the hospital, he named her "Ngang" which means salt. His heart was full of joy because this was his second daughter.

"She will be my last child," he said happily. That year, it was not only a celebration of the end of the harvest season but also the joy of another baby girl in the Zahn family.

Ngang grew up to become a playful and intelligent young girl. She had brown eyes, very dark skin, and coarse hair that was always cut short because she would not let a comb go through it. She enjoyed playing and putting smiles on peoples' faces. She was always helpful, especially to the elders in the community. Every day, she would visit the old widow down the street and help her fetch water, as well as do some of her chores. After, she would go and play with her friends. Her good heart, respect and friendliness were greatly admired, and she grew to loved by everyone.

When Ngang was eleven years old, Mr.Zahn's farming had given him enough capital that he was able to open different businesses in his community. Mr.Zahn also built a new house and every year, he continued to throw the yearly thank you feast where he would thank his ancestors and the God in heaven for blessing him and his family for another year. His grandchildren also participated in the feast , as of his children had married and they attended the feast with their new families.

Ngang was ready to attend secondary school. Mr. Zahn, had a special bond with Ngang and he was willing to send her thousands of miles away where she was to attend a boarding school controlled by the missionaries. He loved his last child so much and he was terribly sad to let go of her, but every time he looked at her, he felt the need to give her the best. By the time Ngang was of secondary school age, the Ngang family had become one of the most influential in the town and Mr. Zahn could afford the best for his last child. One evening, Mr.Zahn called his wife and Ngang to his room. He told them of his intentions to send Ngang to the boarding school, that was four hours away.

Ngang pleaded with him. "Papa , can I please attend secondary school here at home? I don't want to leave the family."

Mr.Zahn was firm. "Mama, it is for your own good. You will make new friends and we will visit you very often. You still have a year to prepare for secondary school."

Ngang turned to her mother. "Mami, please talk to Papa. Who will help Grandma down the streets with her chores? She is getting very tired these days and she will be needing a lot of help."

Mrs.Zahn replied, "Don't worry about her, Ngang. You still have a year before secondary school and when you leave, we will ensure she gets the help she needs."

"Mama, you can now go to your room. Close the door behind you," her father said.

Ngang walked outside the quiet room with a long face. She shut the door behind her but she was curious to hear what the discussion would be once she was outside the room. She stood quietly with her ear pressed to the door. She heard her mother's soft voice. "My love, we have never done this with any of our children, why do this for her?"

Mr.Zahn replied, "I am able to afford an education for her ,and I also believe she would excel at it."

"I am concerned about the fact that she is so young," Mrs. Zahn said. "But If you think is a good idea, let us give it a try."

Ngang moved away from the door to her room. Her only hope of convincing her father had failed and she knew for certain that she would be headed out to the boarding school next year. This was a tough decision for the Zahn's because it was the first time they were sending any of their children away for school, but Mr.Zahn had the conviction that Ngang was meant for this. Months went by and Ngang was ready for secondary school. She told everybody in the community that she would be going and that she would only be at home during the holidays.

The morning came to leave for school. Ngang, her parents and siblings got into the car and headed out for the four-hour journey to her new school. On their way, they stopped at a car park to have good family time. They spent some time eating, drinking and reassuring the baby of the family that she would be visited every month while she was in school. When they arrived at the campus, they were ushered into a building occupied by other girls and their family members.

Bimbia

I couldn't believe that I was actually in a boarding school. I kept looking around to see if I could find someone familiar that could be my friend in this strange place. My brothers carried my little trunk to a corner in the room we had been directed to by the lady at the door. A girl who looked a little older than me walked up to us, asking if I was Ngang Zahn. She introduced herself as my senior student and told me she would be checking my trunk to make sure I had everything the school required from me.

My mother opened my trunk as the senior student went through a list. After being checked in, I was directed to my dormitory where I dropped off my belongings and quickly walked with that senior student to another room to get my uniforms. An older lady helped me try on a uniform, then handed me six different ones in green, blue and orange and asked that the senior student help me put my names on them.. My family spent the whole day with me and later that evening, when all the families were asked to leave, I walked to the gate and waved at them until I could no longer see their car.

Tears rolled down my cheeks. I had held back my tears all day because I didn't want to make my mother feel bad seeing me cry. As the tears continued, I felt a hand on my shoulders. It was the senior student who had been with me all day. Her name was Yvonne but I was to call her Senior Yvonne. "Wipe your tears ,you will be okay here" her soft voice ringing in my ears.. Holding my hand, she took me to my dormitory.

It was a day full of activities and it was finally time to go to bed. The bell rang and all the girls began to change into their pajamas. It was fun being part of an organized system. I climbed up to my metal bed, excitedly imagining my future in the boarding school despite the sadness of being away from my family. Would I have friends? Would the food taste good? Would I be able to spend seven years of my life in this place? Would I excel academically? In the midst of all these thoughts and excitement, I finally fell asleep.

The bell woke me up at five AM the next morning and I followed the other girls to get ready for the day. We had to make up our beds, clean the dormitory then get ready for a shower. Another bell was rung , and we went to the hall for devotions where we sang some hymns, a morning devotion and said prayers. Then the principal made some announcements before breakfast. After breakfast, we went to class, then lunch, siesta, cleaning, evening devotions, prep time then bedtime.

That was the routine for most of the days at the boarding school. My favorite days were Saturday mornings, especially the last Saturday of the month. I enjoyed cleaning and having the best of breakfasts over the weekends. During the week, everything seemed rushed and time was a luxury. Come weekends, the breakfast time was an hour longer and a truck came to the campus with baked goods we were allowed to buy. My friends and I would fill up our breads with sardines and our tea was packed with ovaltine and sugar. I enjoyed every moment of eating a fancy breakfast.

On the last Saturday of every month, I also got more food items from home. I looked forward to the garri, the fried ground nuts, and the sugar to make me a bowl of soaked garri, which was my favorite snack while in school, as well as spending time with my family members that were able to visit me that month.

Four years went by and I was fully incorporated into the boarding school life. One day, I got a message that Miss Smith needed me at the missionaries' office. Without hesitation, I ran out of class to her office. Miss Smith was a woman in her mid-thirties who had spent ten years as a missionary at the boarding school. She first came as a visiting missionary and after that initial three-month experience, she returned to Cameroon as a full time missionary. Ever since she came back to the boarding school, she occasionally visited her home in the US for holidays. She had devoted the last ten years of her life as a missionary working with the girls and was interested in crafts. She was in charge of the sewing /handcraft class and most of us signed up for her classes because she had us sew beautiful pieces. I would spend most of my Sunday afternoons with Miss Smith at the crafting club. I had become one of Miss Smith's favorite students and it was not surprising to have me summoned to her office because we regularly planned the club events together. There was a rumor that she was ready to go back home to the US. During her last visit to the US, she had met a man and they were both committed to getting married and starting a family.

When I got to Miss Smith's office, I was greeted with her usual smile but instead of Miss Smith sending me to the back of her office to arrange the supplies for Sunday's club meeting, she asked me to have a seat. That was unusual and I started feeling like there was something wrong.

"Ngang, I am sure by now you must have heard the rumors that I will be travelling back to my country permanently come June," she said. "I have really enjoyed my stay here but, I have to go back and start a family with my fiancé."

Feeling disappointed at the news I said "Oh no, who's going to head our crafts club? I really enjoy the things we get to make and now that you are leaving, I guess the club will end," I said.

"Unfortunately, the club might need to end, but we have time to train somebody to help the girls out with the club. The other teachers can take charge of the sewing club."

"Miss Smith, I am really going to miss you!" I said, trying not to cry. "Please make sure you keep in touch. Sadly, after next June, I will no longer be attending this school. I will be leaving for high school and my father says it will be in my city because he is getting old and he would like to have his children around him. I will give you our post office mailing box. Please send me letters." I stood up from my seat, ready to leave.

Miss Smith asked me to sit back down. "Ngang, the reason I called you here is to ask if you are interested in coming with me to the

United States. I can apply for you and with the consent of your parents, I can take you along with me so you can further your studies."

I stared at her for a moment, her words running around in my head like playful kittens. She wanted to take me with her? To the United States? I couldn't believe what I was hearing. My eyes were fixed on her beautiful blue eyes and her very white teeth as I watched her lips open and close, and although I was physically present, my thoughts were filled with imaginations of me living in the United States.. This must be a dream! I continued to imagine and although her words were running through my head, I already knew going to study in the United States was something I would love to do.

"Miss Smith." I managed to find my tongue. "I will need to talk to my father about it, but I would really like to come to the United States with you!"

Miss Smith smiled at me with such warmth I had to stop myself from leaping up and hugging her. A light breeze blew in from the window, bringing smells of trees and soil, the familiar aroma of the school where I had spent the last four years of my life. The blind was blowing up and down and it seemed to me that nature was approving of me traveling abroad. I wished she could see the joy in my heart, but I'm sure she could tell because I was shaking on my seat and smiling so widely that anyone looking at me would know I was overwhelmed with happiness.

"You will be called my adopted daughter," she said. She folded her hands on her lap, the ring on her finger glittering in the light. "In two weeks, when you head home for holidays, I will come along with you so we can discuss with your parents the possibility of you traveling with me. You can now go back to class; your geography class should begin in few minutes."

As I rose to leave her office, I couldn't help but hug Ms. Smith. Her soft and warm arms were where I would love to stay but I had to run back to class. Hugging her, I said, "Thank you!"

As I left the office, I saw some of the other girls glance my way. I felt proud, different. I had been offered a gift that I barely understood. Yet, I was also torn with longing for my family and my home - but in that moment, the joy of being asked to travel filled my heart.

I could barely sleep that night. I spent the night thinking of what life in the United States would look like. We had heard stories from the missionaries telling us they sometimes had snow and it got so cold that you had to wear many layers of clothes to feel warm. We had also seen pictures with tall buildings, none of which I was familiar with, especially growing up all my life in a rural area. In the pictures we had seen, I admired the outfits of the girls and wondered when I would get a chance to dress in the same manner. Being in the craft class had made me passionate about fabrics and putting clothing together. Whenever I went home for holidays, I looked for opportunities to wear my handmade pieces and to blend the colors.

Would my father let me travel? Even if he lets me, how am I my supposed to survive without the support of my family? Would I be able to fit in? I had so many questions, my mind was spinning! Maybe, here was my opportunity to become a doctor, a diplomat, a lawyer, a singer, or maybe even an actress! I tossed under my blanket ,would I be able to make new friends? Would I survive all the four seasons? I knew for sure if I travelled, I would love to come home every holiday and visit my family and my friends.

And in the midst of all this, I couldn't help but wonder why Miss Smith had picked me. I felt lucky and I waited in anticipation for the last two weeks of school for my parents to get the news from Miss Smith. Miss Smith had become a family friend over the past years. Whenever my parents were around visiting, they made it a point to see Miss Smith. They sometimes brought gifts for her and my parents knew that she had become my family while I was in school.

Two weeks went by slowly and finally it was the last day of school. Miss Smith had informed my parents that she would be bringing me home so that she could finally get a chance to visit my family at our home. At her arrival, the family welcomed her with a large dinner party, and she spent the night without mentioning why she was there.

When we arrived that night, I confided in my mother the reason why Miss Smith was visiting. Surprisingly, my mother hugged me tightly and whispered in my ear, "I knew from the moment I had you that you would go places. You are my whitewash and you will definitely be a blessing to us." My mother had told me a story many times about my birth. After she gave birth to me, my father's business had prospered and they built a new house, opened up a store and were able to buy cars just within months of me being born. Her mother -my grandmother - had named me "whitewash" , like a paint you use to cover up a newly built house when you can't afford too much of fit. It brings beauty to plainness.

Dreams

The cocks crowed and it was the dawn of another day. Miss Smith mentioned to my father that she would like for them to have a conversation. As per our custom and tradition, if you have a special guest, you invite your family members to welcome the guest properly. My brother was asked to invite my uncle who lived down the street to come over for dinner at our house with his family. My mom spent most of her day in the kitchen preparing the best dishes, with my sister and I helping. We prepared fufu, soup, goat meat, and snails, which was one of Miss Smith's favorite dishes, as well as some jellof rice. Around 5pm, my uncle and my cousins arrived. The two men were seated at the head of the table and my mother said a prayer. The children took their food and sat in a different corner of the room as I was busy telling my siblings and cousins about my last term in school. As the years had gone by, everyone knew my school routine, but they were always curious to know if I was amongst the top five in my class.

After dinner, the elders sat outside to have an adult conversation. They opened the front door and the boys carried four standing chairs to the veranda. My father enjoyed having meetings outside at night because he liked looking at the moon. My mother had told us a story about the woman in the moon, carrying her baby on her back. She said the woman went to the woods to fetch firewood on a Sunday and God was angry at her. He placed her in the moon to serve as an example to community. The lesson was to rest on Sundays and not to perform any hard labour on Sundays. The smell of the beautiful flowers in front of the veranda made sitting outside enchanting, especially at night when the smell of the flowers would saturate your nostrils.

My mother, my uncle, Papa and Miss Smith all sat together to discuss her plan for me. I knew what the purpose of the meeting was and as I sat with the other children my mind was busy trying to figure out what Papa's reaction would be. I could see my mother's face from where I was sitting, and I was hoping that her facial expression would give me a clue as to how the conversation was going. Then I heard my mother called for me to bring a stool and sit beside her. I quickly dragged a wooden stool from the kitchen to the front of the house.

Miss Smith spoke first. "Mr. Zahn, thank you for welcoming me to your home these past couple of days. I have become a friend to the family for the past four years through your lovely daughter Ngang. She is like a daughter to me. The main reason I am here is to inform you that I will be leaving for my country next year at this time. I have really enjoyed the beauty of your country but my fiancé and I have decided to get married and have kids. I feel it's time for me to go back home."

Still not convinced that this was the reason she had visited my family, the men looked at each other with anxiousness. Was this why she took the four-hour drive to visit my family?

Miss Smith continued talking. "The main reason I am here is to ask you for your permission to take your daughter Ngang with me as my adopted daughter. I know it is a tough request to be granted, but I see in your daughter a young woman with great potential in the world. If she comes with me it will be thousands of miles away and yes, it is a different culture for your daughter. However, sir, I promise you, the Lord who has placed this idea in my heart will surely protect her and bring her success wherever she goes. I do not expect you to give me an answer right now, but is it possible for me to have your response by October? If it is a yes, I can get her paperwork ready by June for us to leave for the States together. Please take your time to think about it and thank you for granting me audience."

My father sat quiet for a couple of minutes and every eye was looking at him waiting for him to speak. He had his head down for a couple of minutes, then suddenly looked up at my Mami with a face as if he just heard about my death. He again put his head down and when I saw my Mami's hands reach out to his, I started fearing his response. When he looked up, his eyes red, he took a deep breath, cleared his throat and began speaking to Miss Smith.

"I have heard what you have said, Miss Smith. Thank you for finding our daughter worthy of this huge favor. You must know, I am very concerned about sending my daughter with you. She is a woman. I want her to go to school but at the same time, I cannot allow her to forget her culture. Soon she will need to get married, have children. Where will she find a man from our people over there? Whom will she marry? Let me take some time to discuss this with my people. We will surely get back to you very soon. For now, I am sure your dinner has left your belly. I had one of the hunters get you the best bush meat since this is your last night with us. My wife has made you the best pepper soup. Let us eat and thank the stars for the numerous blessings they bestow upon us."

I kept looking at my mother's face as stared at her husband, and it was difficult for me to tell from her facial expression if she was happy or sad. Every time my father spoke a word, he looked at his brother and with a high sense of approval, my uncle kept nodding his head as he agreed to every word that came out from my father's word. I was dismissed from their presence and as I picked up my stool, I felt deep disappointment at not getting a response.

Two months went by with no word from Dad about the possibility of me traveling abroad to study. He had numerous meetings with his kinsmen and my mother to get their opinions about the issue. My mother was in favor of me traveling abroad and she kept assuring me that my father would definitely come around.

Mami had always admired women who had a career. Unfortunately, she grew up in a poor family and by the age eighteen, she was betrothed to my father. She had married a man who, although uneducated, had a vision of providing the best for his family and unborn children. He had promised Mami that she would be his only wife and although he was under pressure from society to take another wife he remained faithful to her and together they built a successful family and business that became the envy of the town. My mother would make us read to her sometimes and as the years went by, she taught herself how to read. Her pride came from seeing her children receive the best education, a privilege she was never able to attain. My mother had two daughters, my sister and I.

My older sister was married at the age of twenty-one, and she did not get a chance to attend college. My mother had fought so hard against the marriage, but my sister was so in love that she was ready to get married at any expense. Reluctantly, the family gave in.

My five brothers were in charge of the family business and my mother was happy because managing the business amongst the boys kept the family united and closer to home.

I was different, they said. I was born at a time when the education of a girl child was no longer a luxury. My parents promised to give me the best in terms of education and life. My mother would take me to most events with her and during our walks, she would tell me her stories of her childhood and her wish for a better education. She prayed I would excel and make her proud. No wonder, when the opportunity came for me to be educated in the States, she was determined to make sure I held onto it.

The months continued to fly by and yet we had no conclusive word from Papa. My sixty-six-year-old father was worried about letting his fifteen- year -old young and naïve daughter travel abroad. He was afraid; What if she never comes back home? What if she loses her culture? We had medical schools at home and Papa did not see the necessity of me travelling to a foreign country. What if I die, she will not be around during my last days? Papa had always focused on the importance of family and togetherness and because he had worked so hard to provide for his family, he did not see the need for another individual offering to help sponsor his daughter. Papa enjoyed the fact that his children and grandchildren were minutes away from home ,but this was not going to be the case if I was allowed to travel.

The days become months of waiting for Papa's decision. I returned to school in August for the first term in form five and still no response from Papa. Ms. Smith had confided in me her concern that Papa would not let me travel, yet she was hopeful. When Papa and Mami came to visit me in November, they called for Ms. Smith as usual. As the four of us sat together, eating the fried chicken and Dodo Mami had brought, Papa cleared his throat and as if we had made an order, the whole crew looked towards his direction.

Papa " Ms Smith...clearing his throat again.....I have decided Ngang can travel. We are willing to help financially and do not hesitate to contact us for nay assistance"

Fried chicken had never tasted better and as I took a drink of my Fanta, the sweetness was a replica of what my heart was feeling. I thanked my father and in the joy of the moment, we all laughed for the remainder of the two hour visit.

In June of 1996, Miss Smith set out for the United States. My paper work was not ready and the embassy had requested more time to look into my case. In the meantime, Ms. Smith went ahead to get situated and prepare for me to join her and the family. I was sixteen years and ready for high school when I finally received a letter from Miss Smith that I was going to travel as an international student because the adoption request was denied. We had all the paperwork ready and I was granted a visa to travel and study.

That fateful October morning, my parents, siblings, nieces and nephews accompanied me to the airport. I hugged each one of them before departure and when it came to my father's turn, I hugged him tightly with tears streaming down my face ,thanking him. I sat at a window seat and for most of my journey, I was busy looking through the windows and could barely sleep.

"This is no longer a dream," I said to myself. "I'm really leaving to study abroad"

I recalled one of my conversations with Ms. Smith where I expressed my indecision about my future career. She said, "You will be great at whatever you do, Ngang, don't ever lose touch with yourself and your culture. You are unique and you will figure your way through life."

These words rang in my head as I made the long journey that was to change my life.

Reality

On October 8th, 1996, I arrived the United States. Ms. Smith and her fiancé, Uncle Paul, were at the airport waiting for my arrival. We collected my luggage and headed for Virginia. Uncle Paul was curious to learn about my journey and every time he tried to pronounce my name it didn't sound right, but I knew for sure he was talking to me. I looked at Ms. Smith and we smiled at each other because of his funny pronunciation.

As tired as I was, I was too excited to sleep. The frequent yawning, teary eyes and fatigue were a minor concern to me compared to the beautiful tall buildings I was seeing throughout our drive. The unique tall brown trees and the empty branches caught my attention and, as if I was tied to my window seat, I did not want to miss the beautiful scenes during this drive home. However, somewhere between the conversations and my focused gazing outside, I felt asleep and only woke up once we arrived home.

When we arrived at their home, I was welcomed by Uncle Paul's family, but I was so tired that Ms. Smith suggested that I go to sleep. She got me ready for bed and I slept for twelve hours. The first thing I did the next morning was speak to my parents over the phone. They had bought a fixed phone especially so that I could reach them often. I told them about the long flight and how, everything looked different from home. It was cold and I had worn some very thick clothes that morning. I was glad to be in the United States and I could not wait to start school come January.

One afternoon ten days after my arrival, I walked into a fast food restaurant to order some lunch. I had a twenty-dollar bill in my hands and wasn't sure what I was going to order. The cashier walked up to the register.

"May I help you?"

Looking up, I saw numbers next to meals, so I decided to pick a number. He asked, "Is that all?"

Uncertain, I said another number, and he asked again if that was all. I said another number, and a drink. By that time, I was holding out my money.

"Hon, your order's over $20," he said.

I asked him to take out the last one and then he asked was it for here or to go, when I said for here, he looked at me with surprise. "Hon, I'll put your orders in boxes in case you don't finish them so you can take them home."

I smiled and feeling embarrassed, I thanked him and carried with me the five little boxes he had placed on a tray for me. The French fries were all I could eat while I drank the coke. I had no idea how much I had ordered and as I walked home with the leftovers in my two hands, I smiled at my first experience ordering at a restaurant alone. I recounted the story to the family that night. I was under the impression that asking me "is that all?" meant I needed to ask for more stuff which is why I kept adding to my order. We all laughed at my story and there were many more of such experiences to come.

The months and years went by quickly and Uncle Paul and Miss Smith had two lovely daughters, Virginia and Susan. They were my best friends. Virginia was three years and Susan was almost a year old when I was ready to head out for college. Uncle Paul and Ms. Smith did not want me to go away from home, and I decided on a college about three hours away. At the university, my major was in history with a minor in political science.

In the four years of being in the university, I managed to visit Cameroon once during the summers and was excited to reunite with family. My nieces and nephews were all grown up and my parents were getting older by the day. The feeling of missing home seemed to have disappeared over the years and by the time I was heading for my final year in college, my calls back home had now reduced to monthly compared to at least three times a week during my first three years being gone.

Life had gotten so busy for me. I had to meet deadlines with papers as well as other school organizations where I was fully involved. Life was busy yet interesting and in the middle of my busy life, my roommate and I became best friends.

Manal was born in the United States and her parents had immigrated from the Middle East. She aspired to become a doctor and I was interested in becoming a lawyer. We studied and did almost everything together except for classes. During our junior year, we rented an apartment out of campus and stayed as roommates. During most of her short breaks, she would spend it with me and my family in Virginia because she did not want to fly back to California where her family lived.

Manal became my sister and friend. We couldn't wait to graduate and apply to the same graduate school. We hoped we would get into the same school to stay roommates. I had a 70% scholarship to study law at a university in Boston and that was appealing to me as an international student. I couldn't resist the opportunity to attend graduate school at almost no cost.

After our graduation, we took a trip to Virginia Beach and made a promise to stay best friends. I spent my summer relaxing at home with my younger sisters and family. We took road trips and the family wanted us to have really good time before I headed out for graduate school. This was the first summer I did not get to visit Cameroon as I planned for my transition to graduate school.

At twenty-three years old, my life was all figured out I was making my family proud and could not wait to become a lawyer. On August 13, 2004, we were just waking up for breakfast when I heard the phone ring. Uncle Paul answered the phone call.

"Take heart and we will get back to you soon," I heard him say.

He immediately asked me to continue making pancakes for the girls while he went upstairs looking rather strange. I knew there was something wrong. Maybe one of his patients had died? He would sometimes get calls from the hospital at home and that would make him emotional, but not to this extent. I hoped everything was okay at work while I continued making pancakes.

Later that morning, Ms. Smith and I had planned to go out on a girls' trip since I had barely two weeks before beginning graduate school. After I had taken the girls to the bus stop, I saw Uncle Paul and Ms. Smith sitting in the living room talking, severe expressions on their faces. I knew there was something wrong. I knew it couldn't be a patient. I was filled with unease, but went to my room to get ready for my day with Ms.Smith. I came downstairs and found them in the same position, with Ms. Smith still in her pyjamas.

"Is everything okay? Uncle Paul, no work today? Is there another doctor covering for you at the clinic today?" I asked.

"I already called off, Ngang. Everything is fine," he replied.

"Ngang, please come here," said Ms. Smith, opening her arms. "We got a call this morning from Cameroon that your dad has passed away. I called them back after Paul gave me the message and confirmed with your mother and siblings. This must be tough for you, Hon, but we are going to make sure you make it back home to at least attend your father's funeral. Your siblings are not sure yet how long before the burial but in the meantime, sweetheart, be strong and brave. We are here for you."

With my head on Ms. Smith's legs, tears rolled from my eyes. As she spoke, I tried to contain my emotions. It felt like a dream to me. I had spoken to my father just a week ago. He had complained of feeling tired lately. I assured him it was okay for a man in his seventies. The last time I visited home was last year, and my goal was to visit home the following summer. I was thinking that I would spend my first summer of law school at home with my family. My last conversation with my dad was about staying strong and how I would continue to make them proud. He was looking forward to when I would graduate from law school so he could come visit. I remember him looking forward to being on a plane for his first time when he made the trip for my graduation.

My father was a man of honor, and respect and all that mattered to him was family. From a very young age, I had learned the importance of family. Most evenings, my father would gather all his children and ask us individually how we spent the day. Every evening, he would ask my mom last with a big smile and when my mom was done talking, they would wish all of us good night and together holding hands, would go their room. I had always enjoyed how my father treated my mother with so much respect. He saw her as a blessing, and he would surprise her with the finest linens and jewelry. They had been married for more than forty years and the last time I visited, nothing had changed. Even when my nieces and nephews were born, he would have them over most Sundays and ask everyone at the table about their week. He was a man who wanted the best for his children. Not much was said about my grandfather. My father had worked so hard that by his death, he had become a popular businessman and the family business was now run by my brothers. The thought of losing my father and not being around to support my family was scary.

I was his favorite child and that was because he saw in me so many similarities to himself. He was proud of the fact that I was willing to take risks. The last time I visited home, his last words to me were, *keep making us proud, and you are my love.* He gave me a big kiss, wiped his eyes and said, "See you soon."

I recalled the timeless moments I spent with my father. He would tell me a story and at the end, he would ask me what lesson I had learned from it. Once a week, he would have me cut his long nails and this was the time he used to tell me the stories. As a child, I would sit by his legs and watch him play drafts with his friends and brothers and as I grew older, I had mastered the game enough that I began to play with my dad. The bond between us grew stronger by the day and my greatest challenge being away from home was not being close to my parents.

I had to make a brief trip back home for the burial of my father. On the morning of his wake my siblings and his grandchildren were dressed in black and my mother was covered in a white dress. We got into the car and drove to the mortuary. At the mortuary, I snuck my way in to make sure my dad was really dead. Then my eldest brother noticed me amongst the crowd and asked me to leave the room.

"Ngang, you have to leave the room now, this place is meant only for the elders".

I looked at my mother's pale , swollen red eyes and I could tell her soul was broken ,so I let go of her hands that I was tightly holding and walked back outside to meet the rest of the crowd. From the mortuary, we travelled to our town. The next morning we embarked on another four-hour drive to the village where Papa was buried. When we got to the entrance of my village, Dad's coffin was carried by some men on their shoulders and we all walked to our compound. All you could hear in the midst of the music were people sobbing and crying.

Anger, lack of fulfillment and worthlessness filled the moment. All that I had ever done and continued to work hard toward had been to make my parents proud. I was angry at myself and at life. How could my father die without enjoying the fruits of his labor?

Growing up, I was taught to acknowledge the importance of showing appreciation to your parents as they get older. I have lived my whole life with the goal of being able to show appreciation to my parents in their older age.

Two years later, I became an orphan. They said my mother could not take the pain of losing my dad and a year after my Papa's death, she fell sick and died abruptly after a short illness.

In the middle of the semester, I could not travel home for the burial and the only thought that kept me going was the assurance that my parents would have wanted me to excel in school. The guilt of not making it to my mother's burial became the motivation for me to work even harder.

Love Lessions:

I grew up wanting to be loved because love was all I knew. My family members and friends showered me with so much love that I expected that same amount of love from everyone I met in life. Sometimes the love was returned because of what I could offer, other times it was genuine love. Life is good when people treat you right and that was my expectation and philosophy about life. That was short lived.

In my past relationships, I had little to contemplate because I barely remembered what they were about or what transpired in those relationships. These romantic relationships were short lived and break-ups for me were the norm. Before Kevin, my longest relationship was six months and in those six months, I only met up with the guy about six times. In honesty, commitment was not on my mind because I was too busy figuring out my immigration status as well as my career path which deterred me from focusing on a relationship.

My first real relationship was when I met Kevin during graduate school. Our journey began one evening at an international student event on campus where students from all over the world were invited to meet up for a pizza and games night. Manal had persuaded me to go with her. We stayed as roommates in graduate school as well and although we barely saw each other, we tried to make the most of our times together. I reluctantly accepted her request. I would rather have stayed home and watched a movie than walk three blocks down the road for pizza. I committed to going an hour with her, so we wore our jackets and headed down the street, running and laughing so we wouldn't miss out on the pizza.

We walked into the hall and there were about eighty international students from around the world. Walking in, there were decorations from different cultures and international music playing in the background as the students made their way to their seats. Every student wore a traditional outfit. I recognized a few of my friends whom I had met on campus from different parts of Africa. The welcoming party for international students was said to be one of the biggest parties on campus. All international students and students of immigrant parents always looked forward to this event to meet and make new friends. There was a tendency for students from similar cultural background to hang out together and this was not different at my campus. The international student director gave a welcoming speech after which the chaplain gave an opening prayer. It was an evening of fun and four hours passed by and I was still not ready to go home.

I needed some coke to cool off the heat from dancing. At the fountain was a handsome and very dark young man getting a drink as well. He handed me a cup and before I could thank him, he began to speak.

"You should try out the Fanta, every time I drink some Fanta, it reminds me of home," he said.

"Sure. Where is home for you? I am from Cameroon."

"Cameroon too?" He smiled at me. "I am Kevin. You don't sound like you just came to the US?"

"No, I've been here since I was 16. This is pretty much home for me."

We walked away from the fountain and looked for a quiet corner where we spent most of the evening chatting instead of joining the rest of the crowd playing games. That was how I met Kevin. Little did I know that my life was to change, as I would spend the next years of my life loving this man.

I met Kevin during his last year in graduate school of architecture. He quickly became my study partner, mentor and role model. Something about his intelligence was charming and coupled with the fact that we had the same cultural background made him more appealing as a lover. Upon graduation, he got a job that enabled him to travel internationally and this was rare. Everything about him seemed perfect and well planned. His success overshadowed any weaknesses and my admiration for how successful he was dictated the path of our relationship.

"Love is not enough," they say. "You need more than love to marry a man. You need a man that can protect, provide and cherish you."

I was of the other school of thought, which is that love is the most important thing of all. If you give your heart whole heartedly, everything else will fall in place. I have had love so unconditionally given to me that all I knew was to love earnestly with my heart. I remember growing up and believing that I would find myself a man who would love me unconditionally and with his soul like my father loved my mother.

In honesty, it does not matter what philosophy you go by. Either way, it takes two individuals to be in a relationship that works for both of them. At the end of the day, it is the dedication and character of those involved that can make the relationship work. I spent the majority of my life dreaming about the perfect man, the perfect career and a perfect love. Little did I realize that perfect love comes from a perfect person and I was not going to experience the best of love if I did not work on myself first.

Two years into my relationship with Kevin, during my last year of law school, I began to question my definition of love. Not from my experience of previous relationships, because I barely gave it my all before, I met Kevin. At that time, I was twenty-six years old and I felt I was ready. Ready to be a wife, a mother and to feel fulfilled. Yes, a *wife*. That was all I had longed for and I began to groom myself into this role. I was the perfect girlfriend and a few months later the perfect fiancée in public, but with a broken soul.

Sometimes, you can love the idea of love and forget to love the person you are in a relationship with. The fantasy of a successful man, a good background and a bright future; what else would a girl from Cameroon desire, than to be a success story? Everything had to line-up.

During my last visit home to Cameroon, I had a memorable conversation with my father.

"My daughter, I am still waiting for your husband," he said to me. "I will kill five cows and my biggest goat to celebrate your marriage."

"Papa, that day is coming," I promised him, smiling as I held his hands.

"Remember, Ngang. Success without a family is useless. Do not forget the importance of building a family. I have brought my children up knowing that people are true wealth."

"I know Papa, once I finish law school, I will definitely get married."

He gave me a big kiss on my cheek and a big hug.

I was determined to achieve my life goals. Six months into our relationship, one lonely and cold night, I left my part time job at the library and needed to see my love. I worked at the library to earn some extra cash to help as pocket money as well as to send gifts to my nieces and nephews back home.

That night after work at 11pm, I knocked at his apartment and no one came to the door, although I could hear the TV. I looked through the window, and I could see some plates on the table with drinks. It looked like there were people at home. Maybe he was upstairs, or he had just left his apartment? It was uncommon to see Kevin's apartment dead at that time of the night. He was among the rich students on campus and he would normally have his friends over. He lived alone in a well-furnished two-bedroom apartment and drove one of the best cars on campus. In that chilly weather, I walked to the back of his apartment because it was easier to get a look into his bedroom from the back. Walking to the back, I could see the lights from his room reflected in the yard and I thought he might be studying. This was his last year on campus and although it was a relaxed academic year for him, he was given writing assignments often and that kept him busy. As I made it to the back, I looked up in his room window trying to figure his company , disappointed I saw Kevin in bed with another girl.

They got up soon after and got dressed. It seemed surreal. I was speechless and helpless. Tears rolled down my cheeks, but I held back from crying loudly because I did not want them to notice me. I heard the sound of a car leave his yard and when they were gone, I left heart broken and walked back to my apartment wondering how I had let myself be so disrespected.

He apologized and as Manal would say, he was being young and excited? I needed some time to reflect so I asked for some space. A few weeks went by and I was ready to get back into the relationship. Upon his graduation, he travelled very often, and we would make time to see each other whenever he was in town. He showered me with the best gifts and despite the last incident where he cheated on me, our relationship was almost perfect. However, I began to feel insecure because of our history and when he was not around me, I could not help but think he was with another woman.

Almost two years into our relationship, I had the opportunity to meet his parents a couple of times. They would invite me over during my short breaks from school. Aunty was aware I was in a committed relationship and whenever we visited Virginia for the weekend, she would treat Kevin as the son she never had. My culture and heritage was a big deal for me and if I was to marry, I needed a man that could relate to that.

During Christmas break of my last year of law school, I decided to spend some time with Kevin before heading home. He surprised me with a short trip for the weekend. One evening after dinner and some drinks at the resort, I decided to resign to our room for the night. I woke up in the middle of the night and Kevin was not in the room. I walked to the receptionist to look for Kevin and there I found him making out with a woman in front of the hotel.

This time, I summoned the courage to walk up to them and pull on his shirt. Once he saw my pitiful face, I ran back to our room. He followed me back and all I could remember is that I cried myself to sleep. He said he was drunk. He said they had stayed in the lounge and kept on drinking and partying and he got tipsy.

We came back home to Boston and I had three days before I left for Virginia. One of those nights we had arranged to have dinner at Kevin's parents. I had mixed emotions about the future of our relationship, and I could not wait to leave Boston and have some time alone. When we parked in the driveway, Kevin opened the door for me and held my hands tightly.

Immediately his parents walked out smiling and they were chanting in the dialect *'look at my blessings, here they come'* repeatedly. We walked up the stairs and I called Kevin's mother, Mom. She hugged me tightly said, "My Angel, you always brighten my heart whenever I see you."

I smiled back at her. "Mommy," I said. "I always look forward to seeing you and eating your delicious dishes."

We walked in and she had prepared my favorites; fufu and soup, jellof rice, and chicken. There was also lots to drink. We sat at the table eating and talking. Kevin's dad was very impressed that I was in law school. He told me that I was the future for many African women who were scared to take challenges. We talked about the professors at my university that were his friend. He had made it a point to tell them that I was his daughter and that I was going to marry his son. I was popular amongst my professors, a privilege that I enjoyed thanks to Kevin's parents. Kevin meant the world to his parents.

His parents had gotten married in Cameroon when his father was twenty-three and his mother was eighteen. At that time his father was in the university back in Cameroon. He brought his wife with him to the States in the late 1960s so they could build their lives together. Kevin's dad had a vision for himself and his future family. Therefore, he had sent his wife to secondary school classes and he sponsored her through her education until she became a teacher. Luckily for them, he had a scholarship to study in Britain. He was one of the smartest young adults then in Cameroon in math and computer sciences. He went to Britain for four years to obtain his master's degree, and before his departure, his wife was pregnant.

He came back home four years later to a son who he named Kevin. Little Kevin was their world. Soon after, she was blessed to have had another baby girl. They said her name was Angel.

Angel grew up to be a pretty little girl. She looked like an angel from her pictures. She had the biggest one-year-old birthday party in the neighborhood. Kevin's dad had a job where he had to travel to the US to work on a computer program. She was two years old when he got this job and every time he came back home, he would bring clothing and toys for his kids, especially his princess. She was his love.

They said she started with a mild fever and although she was sick, she was still very active. Kevin's mom had treated her for a day or two and when her temperature would not go down, she had rushed her to the hospital. At the hospital, she was diagnosed with malaria and typhoid and little Angel died a week later in the hospital. Sadly enough, her father was not by her side when she died. He came back home three weeks later heart broken, buried his daughter and was not able to forgive himself for not being there to protect his Angel.

For three years, Kevin's dad continued to travel around the world for work as well as teaching computer sciences in some universities in Africa. At this point, he got tired of not spending enough time with his teenage son Kevin, so he accepted a job in the United States and moved with his wife and son. They moved to the United States when Kevin was eleven and ever since then, their lives had been focused on living the American dream. They invested their best in raising a successful, handsome and focused gentleman. Their family story was an example of success.

Dinner was over and I cleared the dishes and joined the men to continue chatting. All of a sudden, his father walked to his office and he came out with his camera. Taking pictures had become a way of telling a story. He touched my shoulder and as I turned around to look at his direction, his mom shouted, "Oh my God!"

I turned to find Kevin on one knee with a ring in his hand. I had never been so blank and quiet in my life. Everything was happening too fast. I had yet to digest the fact that he cheated on me and here I was with his parents as he proposed to me!

I said yes and called Ms.Smith to inform her, but she was already aware and had given her blessings. That was the night it dawned on me that I was in this relationship for real, no matter the circumstances. Despite his infidelity, I was determined to make this relationship work.

Kevin and I had agreed that we were going to have the wedding after I spent a year staying close to Aunty and her family. I would then move back to Boston after the wedding in Virginia and we would begin our family. I was certain that I was going to stay engaged for more than a year before becoming Mrs. Diaw.

My excitement of getting married did not kick in until I moved to Virginia and started planning for the wedding. The excitement of finding a dress, having my friends as bridesmaids, and choosing colors for the wedding became my second job after regular work hours and during the weekends. Aunty and I would talk about the wedding almost every time we hung out together. I was counting my blessings, marrying a man I greatly adored.

In my relationship with Kevin, I had to cover up for his actions because I was embarrassed, he was cheating on me. I barely told Manal about the cheating episodes and if I did, she would quickly brush over it. I hoped that the few times I had caught him cheating on me were the only times.

How did I identify myself? Could I be Ngang without being in a relationship? In this moment of despair, I loved the woman I became.

You really cannot give love if you are not loved. I wanted to be treated as a queen so I decided that whatever the outcome was, I would learn to treat my man as a king. I would make him feel like my mother made my father felt. I was to be the example. I was driven by my desperation to make my relationship work.

Lost

I earned my law degree and started life at a prestigious law firm in Virginia. The great news I had worked so hard for came before I graduated. I was granted a green card based on my academic excellence. I was motivated to work hard because I wanted to make my parents proud, even though they had both died before I became a lawyer. I had moved closer to home in Virginia so I could be near the Smith's family, especially my adopted sisters who wanted us to spend more time together.

Manal and I had stayed best friends and she had invited me to Florida for the weekend to celebrate my job offer as well as my engagement to Kevin. Manal was going to be my chief bridesmaid and it was time for us to catch up and plan for the upcoming wedding. For the past two years, we barely had time to spend more than a few hours together and we were super excited about the weekend. She was serving as a resident in Florida and was excited to show me the beautiful places in her city.

On our second evening out, we decided to go clubbing. Manal enjoyed dancing and clubbing and I had always tagged along to be company for her. I was being pulled to go clubbing again and the thought of it was annoying because I was not a great dancer. However, I was willing to have the fun that weekend and clubbing was not going to slow me down. Back in college ,I enjoyed watching movies while clubbing was Manal's hobby. She was great at it. At the club, I sat down, drinking as usual while Manal danced with strangers as she normally would do. How could she do it so easily? She could make a party happen with random strangers. I wished I could be like her ,having fun whereever I found myself, irrespective whether or not I knew the people.

I was 28 years old, I had a good career, a perfect fiancé and was in every way very accomplished. I had fulfilled my lifetime dream, which was to have a law degree. I was not an ambassador yet, however I was making a difference in the lives of many who walked into my law firm. Every time I won a case, I would go home and have a celebration as I looked forward to the bonus that would be on my next paycheck. I was in Florida, spending the money I had just earned from winning a case that took us about three months to complete. As I sat at the bar and admired Manal on the dance floor, I smiled at my thoughts and accomplishments. I was certain my parents would be super proud of me. I could feel them smiling down at me from heaven.

These few days in Florida were much needed. I was in bed when the phone rang. It was Uncle Paul.

"Hey uncle, is everything okay? It is 7am."

"Yes, Honey, we had a small issue yesterday. It's your Aunty.

"Oh, no!" I cried. "Please tell me she is fine!"

"Honey, we found her on the floor yesterday evening when the girls and I came back from the movies. We immediately called 911 and rushed her to the hospital." He stuttered and no more words came out of his mouth.

"Uncle, I am listening," I urged him to continue.

"She is currently unconscious and the doctor says she might have had a stroke. They ran a couple of tests and we are waiting for the results. I just wanted to inform you, but everything is okay. We are fine and just pray for your Aunty." With that, he burst into tears.

I decided to rush back home to my family. I had to change my flight to the morning instead of the late-night flight.

"It will be well," I said to Uncle Paul. "The doctors have it under control and I will see you in a few hours. I love you, Uncle Paul."

The call dropped and I told Manal I had to leave right away and why. She reassured me my Aunty was going to be fine. I got myself a flight and quickly headed to the airport.

That flight was the longest flight I have ever had in my life and it was barely more than two hours. I was recently assigned a new case at work and I had scheduled a Skype call with the clients earlier that day but could not make it because of this family emergency. I had hoped to be fully in charge on the case so I could make a big profit. I wanted to save up a lot to open an organization in Africa helping young girls. How would that be possible if I couldn't keep my job because Aunty was sick?

Ms. Smith was more than an adopted mother to me. She had brought me to the United States and for so many years, I was her only child until she and Uncle Paul had the girls. People would joke that she was African too because she took such care to keep me true to my culture. She became friends with any Africans she met and especially Cameroonians because she did not want me to lose my culture. She and I attended most of the Cameroonian events in town, especially on Saturdays. She had ensured that I visit Cameroon every summer and Papa paid for my air ticket. It never felt like I was gone from home because I was always visiting Cameroon. People would wonder how I was so "African" I was despite having white parents. I would tell them that is because my parents were Africans in white skin.

My wedding was a year away and Ms. Smith and I had planned to begin the preparations once I returned from my trip to Florida. Uncle Paul was going to walk me down the aisle, but there could be no perfect wedding without Ms. Smith. Who would help me raise my kids? I had lost my biological mother and Ms. Smith was the Mom I was closer to. She watched me become a woman and she knew all about my relationships. She was my confidante, my support and my mentor. I begged for life to please tell me this was a joke.

I walked into her ward and I saw the girls and Uncle Paul all looking worn out. They all ran up to me and gave me a hug. In that moment without saying a word, we were telling each other that we would get through this. It was good to be home. I felt like my presence was an assurance and I needed to be strong for the family. I was the big sister and I could not afford to be weak in front of the girls. The doctor walked in saying good morning. It had been twelve hours and Ms. Smith was still in a coma.

"I cannot say how long she will be in a coma," the Doctor said. "But we are keeping our fingers crossed because she is a fighter. We are still waiting for some of the results of the tests we ran on her, but her blood pressure was quite high and that could be a possible cause for the stroke. Once she gets out of coma, we will go from there." He gave Uncle Paul a pat on his shoulder and left the room.

We had no idea about Ms. Smith's future. She lay there helplessly, and I wished she could just wake up and walk out the door. It all looked like a dream to me because this was the lady I had been with just three days ago. It all had happened too fast and hopefully it would end faster.

A week went by and Aunty was still unconscious. She had tubes placed all over her body that were to assist her with breathing, feeding and elimination of body waste. It was common to see the nurses walk into the room every thirty minutes. They looked at us with a smile, being supportive without saying a word. Day in and day out, Aunty lay in that bed, helpless, and yet we were hopeful.

The hospital became my office. Ever since the incident, I had been working from the hospital. My job was flexible, and my co-worker James was filling in for me by meeting up with my clients. The nurses and doctors kept assuring us to stay positive. A week became two weeks and I was still waiting for that miracle.

My weeks at the hospital began a journey of self-awareness for me. I wrestled with myself and wondered what I could have done to make a difference in the current situation. In that moment, I began to look deep within. I wondered what needed to change, what could I do to save her life? I began to withdraw from my friends, however I stayed close to James and Manal because they were the only friends I could be vulnerable with about my pain. I ignored phone calls because the more I talked to people about the situation the more I felt helpless. Everyone is willing to talk to you about your challenges but the more I spoke about it, the more it reminded me of my grief. Happiness was far gone in my life and everyday living for me was a routine.

At the break of dawn, I would get ready for the hospital and spend my whole day there till evening, when I returned home looking forward to the next morning. Once I made it into Aunty's ward, I pulled up a seat, sat close to her and gazed at her hoping she would wake up and say a word to me. I listened to music to keep me going and sometimes during the day, I would find myself waking up with my head close to her arms. After nap time, I would take a walk around the hospital and if any of the other family members came by later in the evening, we would all chat and uplift each other to cope with our current challenge.

Being around the hospital made me a philosopher. I needed to understand why certain things happened the way they did. Across the hall from the stroke unit was the pediatric unit. I had never seen little children this sick. I was saddened by the pain they had to go through, yet every time I looked at the playground, I saw these children always smiling and ready to play. I could only imagine their pain and how hard it must be for their parents to watch their babies go through this.

One afternoon, as I was taking my usual tour around the hospital, I decided to go into the playground and take a closer look at the drawings since no one was there at that time. I was looking at this particularly beautiful painting on the wall when a this little girl was pushed in on a wheelchair right across from where I was sitting. The painting was of a mother holding tightly to her baby, and although deep in thought about the picture, I was now distracted by this little girl staring at me as she was being pushed towards the other end of the playground.

We smiled at each other and she had the most beautiful cheek bones I had ever seen in my life. She wore a beautiful green dress and white stockings but she had no hair. Her father pushed the wheelchair while her mother carried her teddy bear and a little bag. She had lost her hair probably from chemotherapy, and from her name tag I could tell her name was Favor. She was let out of her wheel-chair and she walked up to me and handed her teddy bear to me. She seemed to be about two years old and could barely speak. We kept exchanging that baby with each other for about thirty minutes, until her parents told her it was time to go back in. I smiled at the parents and they said thank you and left. In the lowest voice, I remember saying, "Thank you, Favor."

The irony of dealing with a sick loved one is it can either make you a strong believer or increase your disbelief. I had been trying to make sense of my life and I realized months down the road that I was helpless. To the world, I was strong because I excelled tremendously at work. I performed better during my court sessions and my rank-ing amongst my peers was the highest. I had to give my best to my work because that was the only way I got my validation. However, this façade couldn't last forever , and I needed a way out.

My true journey to self began while Aunty was in the hospital. I had been strong until the hours turned into days and then weeks, and I knew for sure that I needed a miracle to make Aunty come back to life. I saw my situation as God trying to teach me a lesson. Honestly, I had never been broken both in the spirit and the physically until my Aunty had the stroke. I was devastated, angry and,helpless. As I began to find the answers, I began to appreciate my life. I wondered what possible reason there was for these little babies to be in the hospital. I saw a family spend days and nights in the hospital with their adolescent child who was managing a chronic disease. You can-not understand life at times, but I learned to appreciate where I was coming from.

I walked into this small, dark room and I was hoping to meet Jesus personally in there. It was the hospital chapel. In the most helpless moments of my life, I fell on the floor and for some reason I was speechless. I had all these things I had hoped to pray about but for some reason, I could not pull the energy to get the words out of my mouth. I kept looking steadily at the altar and I was hoping God himself was going to come down and have a conversation with me. He did not show up, but I felt some relief. Being in that room, with tears rolling down my cheeks and staring into an empty altar was the only relief I needed. I left feeling more confident there *was* a God and in Him there was peace because of the relief I felt being in His presence.

Finally, the miracle came on this summer August afternoon. I had fallen asleep and my head was next to Ms. Smith's hands. I felt someone touch my head in my sleep so I opened my eyes and looked towards the door to see if it was one of the nurses. Seeing no one, I lay back my head and decided to go back to sleep. Again, I felt that touch, and looking up, I saw my Aunty's eyes open. In awe, I stared at her face and kept talking to her, but she struggled to bring out any words. I ran out and got the nurses. I was asked to step out of the room and the door was shut. I was in the hallway with no idea of what was going on and if this was a full recovery, considering the fact that she could not utter a word. There was chaos in the room as I heard the professionals yelling amongst themselves. Unfortunately, I could not make sense of the chaos.

I informed Uncle Paul and the girls and you could feel a sense of relief in their voices. Finally, there had been a miracle. Life would get back to normal. I really missed going to work although my colleagues stopped by at least twice a week after work and kept me company.

The nurses walked in an out and I wasn't sure why no one said a word to me. The girls and Uncle Paul arrived at the hospital and finally the doctor walked up to us.

"This is a miracle," he said. "She is doing okay and she seems not to have lost any of her senses. She is tired and cannot speak but she is aware of her environment . You can go in and see her but please do not overwhelm her. Let her regain her energy. We will see her progress in the next couple of days and from there we will be able to decide what will be the next steps. Again, she is a miracle!" He smiled and left.

As we walked in, Aunty was smiling and I was happy again to see her alive. Excitement, joy and tears were uncontrollable. This surely was a miracle. Seeing her be helpless for weeks and now alive although fragile, I knew there must be a great force at work to have brought this to completion. We were only able to get the clues from her facial expression, but she was definitely happy to see us. With the tubes still over her body, she reached out her frail hands longing to be held. Uncle Paul held tightly to her fragile hands, nodding his head and reassuring her that everything would be okay.

Two weeks down the road, Aunty was sent to rehabilitation. Her speech had deteriorated and she needed assistance with activities like feeding, showering and being pushed around on her wheel chair. The doctor had recommended that having her in rehabilitation could lead to better outcomes instead of taking her home directly. Three months was the shortest expected duration of stay but the time went by fast and she would be coming home for Thanksgiving.

Unforeseen

This would be a great Thanksgiving. Uncle Paul's siblings and their children, my sisters, Kevin and I would all be spending Thanksgiving together. Two days before Thanksgiving, Manal and her boyfriend had called that they would be spending the holiday with us as well. I was excited, especially to have Manal around to help with the cooking.

Thanksgiving meal could not have tasted any better. I wasn't sure if it was because Aunty was alive and laughing, or it was having my best friend and my fiancé with me. Uncle Fred, Ms. Smith's brother, said a prayer and it was just fun seeing everyone happy and sharing stories about their Christmas plans. At some point in the conversation, the topic of interest shifted to Kevin and myself

"So, Kevin. How many guests are you guys expecting at the wedding?" Uncle Fred asked.

"About four or five hundred guests."

"Wow! That's a large crowd," he said, amazed.

"In African culture, when two people are getting married, the whole village celebrates," Kevin explained. The crowd nodded in approval.

"I'm super excited that I will get to experience the traditional part of the marriage firsthand. I have heard so much about the tradition from my sister and husband but it will be an honor for me to experience the beauty," said uncle Fred.

"We intend to get authentic African attire for the whole family, and everyone on this table is a part of that family," Kevin said and the crowd burst into laughter. Manal would joke often that I got the best of Africa. She nicknamed Kevin *'Africa's finest'*. I got used to people telling me what a lucky woman I was for having a man like Kevin who was handsome, intelligent and successful and with time I had come to realize I had fallen in love with the "perfect man".

As the evening went by, Kevin and Uncle Paul were in their corner and he left his phone on the couch. I picked the phone to take it to him when I saw a message from a strange name. We had been dating for five years and during this time we had grown to have mutual friends. I saw a message from someone named Kelly.

"Junior and I miss having Daddy spend my first Thanksgiving with us."

At that moment, I could not put in too much thought into the text message with a full house of people, so I needed to act normal until everyone was gone. The evening felt so long and I was ready for everyone to go to bed so I could face Kevin about the text message.

I woke up the next morning and ready to get my answers. He was getting ready to head out and all I needed at the moment was to get my answers.

"Who is Kelly?" I asked him.

"What are you talking about?" He looked at me, surprised.

"Please stop, I saw the text message yesterday."

"Seriously, there is nothing. She was just joking."

"What do you mean?" My heart began to beat faster

"She is a new colleague of mine and she mistakenly sent that message to me."

I stared at him, the early morning sun lighting his features which were as familiar to me as my own. I wanted so badly to believe him, but he seemed to have trouble looking me in the eye. As he got dressed up, I sat on the bed with my focus on him and my words began to rumble. In that moment , I gathered some energy and walked up to him and said, "You know you can tell me anything. Please do not lie to me."

"Can we talk later when I come back from meeting up with these clients of mine? I arranged a meeting here in Virginia at the last minute when I realized I would be spending Thanksgiving with your family."

"Kevin, you're scaring me." I said loudly.

He gave me a kiss and walked out.

I couldn't remember the last time I had said a prayer but I found myself getting on my knees and asking God not to take Kevin out of my life. I couldn't start all over. I would be twenty-nine years old in three months. I needed to get married, and I needed to have children before I turned thirty. He was my perfect man; he had everything I needed in a man.

Let Kelly not be who I think she is and please help me save my relationship.

I needed to know the truth but I was terrified of having that conversation when he returned from his meeting. That evening, I prepared his favorite meal and asked for a romantic evening. The lights were dimmed, the candles were bright and the romantic music in the background were all I needed to console my desperate soul. For the fear of the truth, I decided to not talk about the topic that night.

On Saturday morning Kevin had to leave for Boston. I couldn't let him leave without hearing the truth.

"Can you tell me who Kelly is for real?"

Kevin coughed and shuffled his feet. "She is, um…"

"Okay love, you have to tell me." I held his hands and I am sure he could my heart beating endlessly.

"I am sorry, Ngang.; I didn't know how to tell you. I really love you."

"I know you do," I said. I could feel the goose bumps all over my body and I was about to lose my patience.

"The truth is, she has my baby. She has my son. It was a mistake. Ngang, you are the woman I love. It happened last fall, I went out with my boys to this house party and I had too many drinks. We spent that night together and a couple of times after that. A few months later…hmmm, no it was two months… I met up with her and stopped it. She called me sometime in February that she was pregnant and that I was responsible. I did a DNA test few weeks ago and yes, the boy is mine."

I stared at him like I just saw my parents resurrected from the grave. I was hoping he was joking and although my instincts had told me he lied to me yesterday, I still did not believe. I had no idea on how to react. I kept staring at him and waiting for this joke to come to an end.

"Please stay with me," Kevin continued. "You are the woman I love, and I promise I will never do this again. I could not bring myself to tell you. I was going to tell you but was waiting for a perfect time."

Five years of my life had been given to this man. I was speechless. My heart pounded and tears ran down my cheeks. How could I face the world? What would I tell my family, friends and colleagues had happened between Kevin and I? The betrayal…

Did Kelly even know I existed? Did my moving to Virginia cause him to cheat on me? I couldn't speak. I could barely think. All I knew was that I had failed and my life was falling apart.

Strength

The next Sunday morning I had promised Aunty that I would go to go to church with her. She was so happy to go to church again after her illness. Church was a place I had not paid attention to for the last couple of years. Ever since I got into law school, other things had become more important. Countless times, I would recall the voice of my father telling his teenage girl, "*You will make me proud, you will go places and will not let me down.* "I had become obsessed with the idea of meeting his expectations to the point where I had almost totally forgotten the power of God. There I was in the front row at church, not sure why I was there. I had to be there for Ms. Smith as she believed God was her healer. I knew for sure her recovery was a miracle, but I wasn't certain if God was fully responsible for the healing. The meaning of God for most of my adulthood had boiled down to ethics – when you invest good in the universe, you will reap good as a reward.

The pastor walked up to the altar and he called out to Ms. Smith. He asked the congregation to stand and welcome her. I had never felt this much love shown to an individual and it inspired me to pay attention to the message.

Phillipians 1:6: "I am certain that God, who began the good work within you, will continue his work until it is finally finished on the day Christ Jesus returns. Brethrens, this verse gives us assurance in our trials. Despite our sicknesses, financial issues, pain and all, stay assured that all things work together for good. God allows everything to happen for a purpose, both the good and bad so that you can be transformed to the image of God. As we leave here today, stay assured that through it all, God is working for your good. Amen".

Tears rolled down my cheeks. How can you know this, God? Does He know what I am going through? Does he know my issues with Kevin? Was he there when Ms. Smith almost died? How is all this working for my good? Aunty and Uncle had their hands on my shoulders as I struggled to wipe my rolling tears. I had never felt this vulnerable in the midst of strangers. I could feel the tears rolling down my cheeks but within me, there was so much joy. I felt relief knowing something good was about to happen in my life.

Please God, I know you are watching over me and please show me the good in life.

The service ended and people smiled and exchanged greetings that took about the same amount of time as the service. I pulled up the car and as I waited for the couple, I reflected on the message, especially figuring out the good in my life.

"Ngang, do you want to tell me what is going on?" Ms. Smith asked.

"Not much. Everything is fine," I told her. I didn't want to burden her with my sorrow.

"It's just two of us at home, I asked Paul to give us the evening. We're going to have a girls' time. This whole house is ours so you better start talking so you can get back to your apartment and get ready for work tomorrow."

"I am fine. Being fully back at work, it is overwhelming," I said.

"How is Kevin?" she asked.

"He is …um … fine. You know him, work as usual. I will be spending Christmas with his family. I am excited." I took the mug she had been drinking her tea from to the kitchen.

She looked at me as if she knew I had lied to her. "Sit down baby. I was hoping to tell you something before your wedding. Do not let the things of the world bring you down. It only gets worst as you get older. You have to stay strong knowing that you have the strength and support to pull through. Don't forget, your name is Ngang. It means salt; you add taste and value to whatever and whomever you meet. I am here for you, my daughter. Thank you for blessing me with your love."

Her gentle and ever so calming voice got the tears rolling again and I began to talk .

"Aunty, Kevin has a son with another woman." I burst out into tears.

She spoke in her gentle voice, opening her arms to hug me. "Come here, baby."

"He said I am the one he loves, and he still wants us to go ahead with the wedding. I have given five years of my life to this man. It could not get any worse. How can he betray me this much? What will I tell people, how will I face my colleagues? The wedding is scheduled for less than a year from now. Aunty, please help me! I don't know what to do. I'm very confused."

"Life throws us challenges, Ngang. You can only face the issues from within. Remember what the pastor said today, it all works together for the good. Baby trust me, it always does. It will seem like the worst thing that can ever happen to you but at the end it will all make sense because you will see the goodness. No man is perfect. When you love someone, you accept their flaws and you are willing to bring out the best in that person. Forget about the world. I know you have always wanted to get married and be a mother. I feel proud because you are very successful. You are not running a race with life. I know you are feeling the pressure, but honey life has a different plan for each of us. You are simply living life and whatever comes your way, you accept your journey. Take a deep breath and make your decision. Baby please, pray. Yes, please pray. Trust God when he is calling you. He sure has greater plans for you that are not clearer now."

"Where did I go wrong?" I asked.

"You don't have to *be* wrong for things to *go* wrong. I know you have been betrayed but maybe you should be looking deep down.

Are you ready for marriage, do you really love this man enough to forgive his mistake? If you do love him, are you going to let his actions dictate your joy? My daughter, as we get older, our battles, our struggles, our worries, our fears, our expectations can only be managed by us. A woman is not completed by the man she marries. You have to see yourself complete as an individual and the man you marry becomes your partner. You do not need any man to complete you. Pay attention to the heart of a man and not the physical looks. You are a successful career woman, but you need to have the completeness in your heart and spirit that you are enough. That will make you stronger and take you through this world. Again, the challenges of life only get tougher. I will make you some dinner before you head home to get ready for work tomorrow. Cheer up and know you are never too old to talk to me and share your thoughts, baby girl."

The holidays came and went and not a day went by without me reflecting on my last intimate conversation with Aunty. I thought that with the education, status and success I had earned, I was ready for whatever turns my life had to take. I had managed to keep my issue with Kevin from the public for the past six weeks and he was mounting pressure about beginning preparations for the wedding. I felt more than reluctant to begin planning and I told him we would begin planning on the first week of February. Deep within me, I was confused if I had really ever loved this man. I was scared of the stigma, especially with my colleagues at work. As the days drew closer to February, I became more and more anxious and unsure about my love for Kevin.

James invited me over for dinner one evening. James and I had bonded at work because we were the only two Africans. James was calm. He had very dark skin and was super intelligent. I always referred to him as the smarter one, even though I was his superior at work. I had just received a promotion and he wanted to celebrate with me. Working with him we had become close and Kevin and I had gone on double dates with him and his girlfriend, Cathy. She was all about his money. As long as he paid the bills and took her on expensive trips, she was fine. I nick-named James ATM, and our friendship was filled with laughter and support for each other.

When I arrived at his apartment, James was busy cooking and setting up the table. I placed the bottle of wine I had brought on the table and helped him with the cooking. Whenever I was with James, there had always been a sense of calm and freedom.

My bag was lying next to him on his sofa, and I reached to get my purse. As I leaned over his legs, I looked up at him and I realized I needed him to kiss. I wanted him to kiss me so badly.

He kept holding back, but I was sure I needed that kiss now and it finally happened. It felt so real. This was what I needed for my lost soul. I woke up the next morning smiling still lying in James' arms. It was the best night I ever had and if given the chance, I would do it all over again and for sure with James.

I rushed home so I could join my parents for church.

"Someone is glowing today," Aunty said.

I chuckled and told her I'd had a private dinner with James.

"I have always known that you two were up to no good," she laughed. She handed over her purse for me to help her with it as we joined Uncle Paul in the car.

Death to Life

January 28th was a dreadful morning. I woke up to the news that my beloved Aunty had passed away. Once the autopsy was done, it was said she had a heart attack. I always felt like she had stayed longer because she wanted to have that special conversation with me. In life, we get to meet people who love us unconditionally and with such love, we find strength to be the best version of ourselves.

All I wanted as a teenager was to eat, play and sleep. As an adult, life throws situations at you that challenge your very existence. At twenty-nine years old, I was an orphan. I had just lost my adopted mother and I was unsure about my engagement. The pain and shame from these losses weighed heavily on me to the point I was about to lose my mind. The shame of not being enough to hold onto my relationship, of not being able to show my appreciation to my biological parents as well as guilt from not being able to help Aunty during her chronic illness was too much to bear. I was under the impression that my predicaments were a result of my misbehavior.

How did your life get so bad? You had it all planned and unfortunately you failed yourself and the universe, Ngang.

My mind was crowded with the worries of the world. I could not take it anymore until I started praying for peace. I couldn't solve all my issues, I couldn't bring my parents back to life, I couldn't understand why this fifty-eight-year-old woman, my Aunty, died from a heart attack. She was healthy, a good woman who loved unfailingly. This didn't make any sense.

God, grant me the peace to live life.

Peace of mind is a luxury that I hadn't had ever since I became ambitious and successful. I was always focused on the next achievement. I thought being a successful lawyer was my life's goal. With that came the urge to make sure everyone in the family was fine. I worried about my family back home, I worried about Aunty and the girls. I had to make sure everyone was fine. This was taking a toll on me.

These past couple of months I had found myself asking questions and seeking more answers from God. Finding scriptures that encouraged me to trust God more, I began to pray for peace of mind. I knew I could not be happy with a life where I wanted everything fixed and perfect. I understood more that it was okay for me to make mistakes and not be in control of everything. However, I still could not make sense as to why my situation was harder and different from everyone else's.

The morning of Aunty's funeral was a cold, bright and beautiful morning. The skies were quiet and the piles of snow on the ground could not have made the morning view more beautiful. There is something about winter mornings , despite their dreadful cold, there is some peace and calmness that comes with it. Ever since Aunty's death, I had spent the last couple of weeks staying at home to help Uncle Paul prepare for her funeral. While the arrangements were being made, I started packing up her things to secure her treasured belongings for the girls and to donate whatever was left. It was frequent to have visitors around the house during these last weeks.

Aunty, I called her Mom for most of my life. She was more than a mentor, a friend, a mother figure, she was also an angel to me. My memories of her role in my life were endless and it was hard for me to narrow her influence in my life to the fifteen minutes that I was allotted to talk during her funeral.

I remembered my first day in a new school with no friends when she stood for about thirty minutes by the door to make sure I was settled in my new class. And when she was worried I would be bullied by the kids in my school because of my accent, she would stop by my school every so often to check in on me. When I had my first job and I came back home frustrated by not understanding what most customers said because of their accent, she told me, "You will get to understand them better with time. Just be patient, honey."

At first when I moved to the U.S with her, I still saw her as my craft teacher. She was that nice lady to me and throughout my teenage years, I would still introduce her as Ms. Smith, which she was fine with. I gave her all the respect she deserved, however at the back of my mind, for years I knew she and Uncle weren't my family. They were a nice family providing me with the opportunity to become a better person and I appreciated their love and trust. This changed when the girls were born. I remember she would tell me, *'Take care of your sisters.'*

I found myself becoming more integrated into the family and the little girls became the little sisters I never had.

I was numb the morning of her funeral . I walked into the girls' room and we sat in bed for a while. They were now teenagers and over the last year, they were psychologically prepared to expect the worst for their mom. We sat in bed talking about Mom and couldn't help but smile with tears rolling down our cheeks.

Once, when the girls wanted to attend a party and we knew she and Uncle Paul were not going to buy into the idea because the party was going to be till 9pm. I had come up with the plot that we were going shopping and I would take them to a late movie so we wouldn't be home till midnight. That evening, when we were about to leave, Aunty had given us some money to use shopping and she said be careful, smiling at us as we left for the mall. The girl's and I got back home late that night and their parents were fast asleep. In the morning, during breakfast, she coughed, "How was the movie last night?"

"Good", I said narrating the movie to her and said we would watch it again.

She and Uncle Paul laughed, "Girls, we know you guys were at that school party last night."

I explained to them that I had stayed in my car and waited for the girls and they were safe. This is one of the many tricks they caught us doing, and we laughed about how they always figured out what we were up to.

We had grown up in a home that was nurturing and filled with love. Our parents were hard workers. They let each of us grow at our own pace, yet they instilled in us the virtue of hard work. My biological parents had always reiterated this virtue to me that I had to be exceptional and that only came by hard work and excellence. I never felt like I was smart enough, but I knew I had to work extra hard to attain my goals. Aunty hated the fact that I was under so much pressure to succeed. She would say, "Honey, hopefully you stay alive long enough to enjoy the benefits of your hard work."

My sisters and I spent two hours in bed talking, and we decided to head out to Uncle Paul's room. We walked in to see him sitting on the couch with a picture of Mom in his hands, sobbing and staring at her .These two people were so much in love with each other and despite Uncle's Paul busy schedule, he made sure he showered his family with love whenever he had the opportunity, especially his wife. When she had the stroke, he took the news fairly well because he was a professional and even on the days he spent sixteen hours at his hospital, he would stop by every day. I admired how much he loved his wife but more importantly how he had a big enough heart to bring me into his home and to love me without boundaries.

We spent some time consoling Uncle Paul and assuring him of our love for him. I headed to the kitchen and prepared breakfast and we all got ready to head out for the viewing and the funeral.

We arrived at the funeral and there was everybody we expected. Manal flew in with her husband, Kevin was there, and James, Aunty's church members, friends, family members, the Diaw's, the girls had some of their friends present as well as colleagues of Uncle Paul. We were welcomed with hugs, kisses and people smiling at us. I knew for sure that Aunty would be happy that her funeral was filled with so much love and I was glad that she lived her life with so much love that she received love even in death.

My life with Aunty was filled with lessons that were the most important ones during my adult years. While she was unconscious in the hospital, I learned the importance of belonging to a community. I grew up in Africa knowing the importance of community. My father would have a big feast annually and my whole community would be at our house to celebrate with my father. I knew almost everyone in my city. I considered every woman in my town and my church a mother figure and I would never pass by an elderly person without saying a greeting. This was different when I moved to the United States. Aunty's sickness showed me the need to belong to a community here as well. The love she poured to her friends, colleagues, neighbors, and church members was overwhelming. I am not sure if, when she was being friendly to these people, she anticipated that they were going to repay her with such an outpouring of love in return, especially during her dying days.

I walked up to the pulpit to give my eulogy. As I stood there I stared at her casket and at the crowd. I did not mourn the death of my parents so much, because I was still showered with the parental love of the Smiths. Other people had spoken, as well as the girls, and I was the last one before Uncle Paul. So, I stood up at the pulpit, speechless and overwhelmed by emotions, yet I had so much to say that could not be said without tears rolling down my cheeks. In that moment, I started singing a song that Ms. Smith had taught us back during our boarding school days in Cameroon titled, "It Is Well". The story behind the song never left my memory and seventeen years later, when words could not make sense, all I had was this song to give me courage.

When peace, like a river, attendeth my way,
When sorrows like sea billows roll
Whatever my lot, thou hast taught me to say
It is well, it is well, with my soul

It is well
With my soul
It is well, it is well with my soul

Though Satan should buffet, though trials should come,
Let this blest assurance control,
That Christ has regarded my helpless estate,
And hath shed His own blood for my soul

It is well (it is well)
With my soul (with my soul)
It is well, it is well with my soul

I took a deep breath, wiped off my tears, then the words began to come out slowly. "My name is Ngang and Aunty is my mother. I met her while I was back home in Cameroon in a girl's boarding school. She was my craft teacher and she could make the most beautiful pieces. She soon became fond of me and that is why she encouraged me to study abroad here. My biological parents must have seen an angel in Ms. Smith when they let their sixteen-year-old daughter travel across the world with a stranger. Angels really do exist and to be loved by a woman of a different color, culture and race so deeply makes me one of the blessed humans to have lived on this earth. Thank you, Dad, and my lovely sisters for loving me whole –heartedly. Mom, you made me the woman that I am today and please bring my regards to my parents. There is a party in heaven today because my parents are there throwing you a big welcome party." The tears continued to roll down my cheeks as I said these words.

Broken

After the burial of Ms. Smith, life could never be normal again. I lost the part of me that felt like I belonged somewhere. I had no sense of closeness to any family; I had become very fond of Ms. Smith and her passing away made me lonely. I spent a lot of time at Uncle Paul's with him on his day off to keep him company while the girls were busy with school. The house felt empty and the pictures of Ms. Smith on the wall only reminded me of a loss so irreplaceable. Every picture on the wall had a story.

One picture was taken on the second weekend of me being in the United States. The couple and I had taken a family portrait and I stared at my long-braided hair, innocent face and excitement about life. I wondered if the sixteen-year-old version of me could recognize the shadow I had become of myself. Lost, lonely and afraid. I wondered where the bold, ambitious and daring version of me had gone.

My Papa's motto when I was growing up was "There is a time for everything". I wondered what time I was facing in my life. Amidst the brokenness, I decided to make a trip to Cameroon. Two weeks after Ms. Smith's burial, I couldn't take the pain anymore and I wondered how much of a help I was to the people around me. As I flew to Cameroon that March evening, I wasn't sure what I was looking for after four years of not being home, but I certainly felt like I had to reconnect with a part of me that could only be found in Cameroon. When I arrived home, all I wanted to do was sleep for the first two days.

My father's house was now occupied by my eldest brother, his wife and children. The seven-room house looked different, however the memories of my childhood were vivid with every step I took in the house. Only four of the rooms were fully occupied. Growing up, our house was always full with at least eleven people living there. We always had extended family members living with us and it was strange to see how things had changed. Every morning when I opened the windows, looking at green leaves on the orange tree which was my favorite spot in the compound and the tall coconut trees behind the house with the sunlight rays directly going through my window, I realized how much I had missed my home. As I looked outside one morning, I heard a knock on my door.

"Ngang, it's me," my brother said.

"Come in big brother." I sat up to listen to what he had to say.

"Ngang, you have not been home since Mom died," my eldest brother said.

"Yes, life has been busy and unfair. But I am home now," I replied.

"Sorry about Ms. Smith's dead. I know she was like a mother to you. How are you doing?" my brother asked.

"I am fine. I just feel lost right now. I'm afraid and angry. Not sure why I feel this way," I replied.

"Hmm, your two weeks here will be very busy. You will have to meet with all your siblings and their children. Our sister is already complaining that she hasn't seen you in two days. I told them you needed to rest," he said.

I smiled and said thank you because my sister could be dramatic and she was probably wondering why I wasn't staying with her family. I just needed to be home, to feel the warmth of my parents and staying at my parents' house was the best option.

"Also, let me know what your schedule is, we need to visit Mami's grave. You were not here for her burial," he said.

"Sure, big brother," I murmured as I lay back down.

"Ngang, I can see you are angry. And little sister, you are now grown up and I wish I could see my baby sister that always made me proud. Don't beat yourself up, remember you have always made us proud. Our people say that a warrior fights with courage and not with anger. Let it go. It is not your fault. That is life for you."

"Thank you, big brother. I feel like I am drowning. I appreciate the concern."

My days at home were packed with activities and time seemed to fly too fast. A few days later, my siblings, their families and I took a trip to the village to visit my Mami's grave. The visit to her grave was more of a party as we all reflected on her funny and memorable stories. She had a way of communicating her point through storytelling and often very funny stories with great lessons.

Growing up in Cameroon, I remember one of the evenings we were sitting outside enjoying the moonlight and listening to my mother tell us stories. One of her stories has stuck with me throughout my life.

"A poor girl got married to the prince of her tribe. After the wedding ceremony, she moved into the palace to live with the prince. One day, the immediate family of the girl came to visit her and sadly, they were not permitted to go into the palace because of their social status. The servant went into the palace and informed her: "Madam, your people are outside looking for you, but they cannot come in because the law of the palace allows only royalty to visit."

She looked at the servant and asked him, "So who do you say I am?"

The servant replied, "Royalty."

Then she demanded the servant to let her family in, saying, "Whomever I have become today, it is because of the poverty I came from."

My mother would then look around at us, her children, reminding us that no matter how successful you become in life, never forget your roots. That is your foundation.

How I missed my parents but to see how strong my siblings were and the love and unity amongst us reminded me of where home truly was. It was time for me to go back to the United States and it felt like I had removed the weight of the world from my shoulders. I had regained a sense of purpose and a reminder that all the misfortunes in my life were no fault of mine. James picked me up from the airport and it was good to be back in the United States again.

As I walked outside the airport, I could smell spring. The bright colored jackets, the smell of flowers, the little drops of rain reminded me that the brutal winter was almost over. James was wearing a black sweater and jeans and I could see his white teeth shining through his dark bold face. As he walked towards me, I walked faster to get into his arms. We were both as excited as if it had been a year without seeing each other.

"Woman, you look great. You were a mess before you left for Cameroon," James said.

"Seriously, I guess I just needed some real African food," I said, smiling.

"Talking about food, can we have dinner tomorrow evening? I am going to let you sleep in today and tomorrow. Your favorite restaurant. Are you in?" James asked.

"I wanted to stop by Uncle Smith's tomorrow. I called yesterday but didn't get hold of anyone," I said.

"Oh yes, I spoke to him last weekend about picking you up today and he said he will be working out of state this weekend. Guess he's not yet back home and you know he is not big with using this cell phone," James said.

"How about the girls?" I. asked.

"They are on spring break with their Uncle "He replied

"Well, dinner it is tomorrow. I need some good drinks," I said.

We finally made it to the parking lot and as we drove home, it felt like I had only travelled for a day. Nothing seemed different yet except for the feel in change of seasons. I filled James ears with stories about how grown my nieces and nephews were, the joy of reconnecting with my siblings and the peace of staying in my childhood house. I had enjoyed the warm weather, the beaches and the warmth of being in the community. Most of my parents' friends were either dead or had moved away. My childhood friends had all relocated to bigger cities and I was impressed to hear about a few of them who had travelled abroad for school. Unfamiliar faces filled every gathering I attended in my city but there was always joy in the midst of these strangers.

On Saturday morning all I wanted to do was sleep. I spent my day sorting out the crayfish, vegetables, dried fish and spices I had brought with me from Cameroon. Uncle Smith and the girls enjoyed goat meat pepper soup and I had brought some spices to make them some. In between the unpacking and cleaning up, I fell asleep again and it was a loud knock on my door that woke me up.

James smiled at me. "Woman, I have been calling your phone for the past two hours ; you got me worried."

"You always worry. Sorry I passed out with the clothes on my bed. Could you help me clean up? By the way, you dressed up. What's the occasion?" I asked.

"Madam, we have a dinner planned tonight. It is one more hour to our reservation. Can you get ready and I will stop by tomorrow to help you clean up?"

"Sure, give me thirty minutes. I'll just get some jeans on quickly."

"No, ma'am, you are dressing fancy," he replied.

I quickly took a shower and wore my favorite green dress I had bought on a shopping trip with Ms. Smith. She saw the dress first and recommended that I get it. It was a long sleeved dark green midi dress with a flare at the bottom. Not too thick to be worn outside without a jacket on a spring evening. The six gold attached buttons were the highlight of the outfit and made every detail on the dress more beautiful. It was usual to get compliments from James and I had my newly braided hair I had done while in Cameroon tied in a bun. My red lips were sparkling, and I walked like a princess in my black high heeled shoes. I was ready for the night, dressed up and feeling relaxed with James.

This part of the city had a unique ambience. The variety of restaurants and the beauty of the buildings was always welcoming. I am a fan of anything with rice and I was looking forward to a heavy dinner with some drinking. We parked the car at the back of the restaurant because it was easier to avoid the lines at the front by coming in through the back. As we walked closer to the restaurant, I commented seeing someone who looked like Manal.

"James, I just saw someone like Manal. She is wearing a pair of jeans."

"Funny how you can make out your friend from afar," James replied

"Well, she can't be in town without letting me know?" I said.

James opened the door for me and as I got in and looked at his charming dark face, I could not help but think how handsome, humble and kind James was. He treated me as one of his little sisters and I enjoyed the feeling I received every time we hung out together.

"Please follow me," said the waitress.

Confused as to why James had reserved a room instead of sitting outside as usual in the open, I stretched out my hand as to hold his shirt when I heard a loud "Surprise" and as I looked to the room on my left, I saw Manal, her fiancé , Uncle Paul and the girls. These were the last people I had expected to see, and James had planned out this perfect evening for me to reconnect with my circle. The warmth, laughter and love I felt was real and I could not hold back the smile and blushing. That was all James and he was magical.

Journey

When I left Cameroon as a child, the excitement was overwhelming. My expectations for the future were filled with prosperity and wealth. I was intrigued by the determination and strength I saw people develop as I grew older to meet these expectations. As I sat on my bed one Sunday morning, I began to reflect on the lives of the many I had been touched by.

James, who was my co-partner at work, had immigrated to the US as a refugee at the age of seventeen. He had lost both of his parents and one of his siblings during the war in Niger in 1990. He had a faint memory of his elder sister who was taken to a refugee camp in Nigeria to be brought to the U.S, while his elder brother was left at the camp in Niger awaiting evaluation if he was fit to travel as an immigrant.

At seventeen years old, James had to hustle his way to a decent life. When he arrived in the US, he lived in a home with refugees from across the world. At the refugee home, with time, he got his refugee status and those who were above eighteen had to start a life on their own six months after their eighteen birthday. A few months after arriving in the United States, James was enrolled in school and he struggled so much with his studies that he was asked to withdraw and enroll in language classes. He spent a year and a half studying English and when he turned eighteen, it was time for him to create room for another refugee, so he made plans to get himself an apartment not too far from the home. His only family were those at the home and he was frightened by the fact that he would have to be alone if he were to move far away.

With time, James got himself a job and life, like he would say, became a race. He would leave school, go to work, complete assignments and find time to hang out at the home. He would walk about two blocks to get the bus, but every morning he woke up with a new determination to succeed. His bus ride was an hour and a half, and every morning he left the house by 7am and got back home by 10pm. The hardest part for him was to learn a new language and be competent in this language. He took language classes for a year and a half before fully enrolling in high school. This was his routine for two years throughout high school until he became a college student.

Despite the challenges, James was determined and excited to become a lawyer and as the days went by his ambitions grew bigger. When he passed his English competency test, he was enrolled in a local high school and he excelled amongst his peers. When he was admitted into college, he was an outstanding student and that made his admission into law school easier for him because he had offers from many schools. James performed extremely well in law school and he had been working at the same company for five years.

With time, he was able to reconnect with his sister who was now married with a family in Nigeria, and in time he was able to sponsor his elder brother to travel to the United States and join him. This was the story of a thirty-three-year-old man who had taken the opportunity given to him and struggled to make his life exemplary. That was the story common amongst many people I knew. Decent living was not handed over to them, it came at the expense of sleepless nights, having multiple jobs and getting off a job at 7 AM and taking an exam at 9AM yet they managed to build their success stories. These are the stories that make you humble, that make you realize the importance of never giving up and dreaming. As a child you dream of the future but when adulthood hits, there is barely a warning to prepare you for the realities of life. I could relate more to James. Although I didn't have to work three jobs and many more of his hustles to succeed, we both had the drive to succeed. To me, success meant living a life better than my parents would have ever dreamt of experiencing for themselves due to the opportunities that were provided to them.

My journey had some similarities with that of James, however I had a family that I could lean on. Originally when Ms. Smith had approached my family, her goal was to adopt me so I would have the full benefits of being in the United States. Unfortunately, that route seemed almost impossible and I finally came in with a student visa. High school tuition was less expensive, and the Smiths made sure I lacked nothing. While in college, my parents in Cameroon and the Smiths paid my tuition which was still not a lot because of the scholarship opportunities I had. My needs became more as I grew older and I had to pick up work to take care of certain needs.

In college during school hours, I was only allowed to work twenty hours a week and forty hours during holidays to keep my visa in good standing. One job I loved having in college was working in the cafeteria. At the end of a shift at the cafeteria, I had a free meal and that would save me the pain of figuring out what to eat. During the summer holidays that I did not visit Cameroon, I would work full time as a custodian on campus or whatever job was available to save some extra cash.

One summer, as I planned a trip to visit Cameroon, I needed some extra money. I heard a hotel was hiring so I decided to apply for the job as a front desk receptionist.

"Are you sure you can work here?" the man at the desk asked.

"Yes Sir, I have experience in custodian services, and I am available most evenings until 11pm. I replied.

"We are hiring but you do not have to do this job." The man looked at me. "If you are looking for more money, you can be my girlfriend; I will give you a $300 every month for your upkeep and I will take care of you."

I walked immediately out of his office scared and vulnerable. I was sure he had seen some desperation in me to have mentioned his offer. But the anger was shockingly short lived because I decided not to internalized his view of me. So, I had to let it go and continue to push forward while hoping for the best. He kept calling my phone and actually increased the offer, butI hated him for trying to exploit my situation. The thought of him disgusted me and eventually he gave up.

I remember when the Smiths presented me with a car for getting into law school. That was one of my happiest days of my life because a car was a luxury to me. I had grown to put emphasis on the end goal and if I could do without, I survived without. Throughout college, I had relied on public transport and Manal for transportation. Upon graduation of law school, because I was the top in my class, I had three job offers and they all came with a work visa. That made my transition to the work world so much easier and it was soothing to know that my hard work finally paid off.

This was the period in my life where although I had attained the dream, the process had shaped me with humility. I have lived in both worlds. I have seen what it means to be a janitor, a student and yes, a lawyer. It gives you a perspective in life where you can respect everyone. I am certain that if I had not gone through those experiences and was now a lawyer, I would not have appreciated the role of God in my life.

For me, I learned that my hard work can only take me so far. I know of people who worked three times harder than I did, who went above and beyond to make things happen and others who lost their mind in the process of making it. Some of them did not have the same opportunities given to them like I did, and their hard work was never brought to light. Then I realized that my hard work was buttered with favor. God must have had a plan for my life. He must have handpicked me because despite the brokenness, tears and despair during my tough years, He sustained me to enjoy success. With this in mind, I am grateful and humbled that the grace of God has favored me. When you become the best version of yourself from being broken, you begin to appreciate the simplicity of life.

Whether you had it "easy" like me, or rough like James, you never forget who you are and where you came from. This is a tough corner to be in because the pressure not to waste the opportunity is heavy on you. Success can sometimes feel empty especially at the cost of tears and sleepless nights. I considered myself the epitome of success until I began to appreciate the little things in life. I began to appreciate having a meal a day, good health, true friendships, life and everyone I came across in my life henceforth was of value to me. This is what you learn from life when you experience tough times.

Expectations

One Monday morning, I heard a loud knock on my door.

I opened the door, surprised to see Kevin standing there. I looked at his pale face and all I could think about was my anger towards him. His hands shivered as he struggled to give me a hug and reluctantly I wrapped my arms around his back We slowly worked our way into my living room. My living room felt like a court room and each party seemed to expect the other to make their case. I offered him coffee.

"Babe, how was your trip? I tried calling you a couple of times, but you would not answer or return my calls."

"I told you, I needed some time to think about my life. A lot of things were crumbling and you were part of it."

"Okay, so I took off time from work for us to work this out. I am sorry," he said.

"How long did you take off from work?" I asked.

"Two weeks. However, I am willing to move closer to you," he replied.

A lack of words and emotions, that's all there was in that moment. I stared at him. A few months ago, I could not wait to become his wife, but at that moment I wasn't even sure if I wanted to spend a day with him. As I struggled to put my thoughts together, the sound of the bell saved me from spilling out the nasty words that were playing in my head.

James was at the door. We had planned to visit a non-profit organization that morning to apply to serve as volunteers. This organization was focused on helping immigrants integrate in their new environment. James came and hugged me. As he and Kevin were catching up, I hurried to my room to get ready for the day.

"Kev, James and I had plans for the day. Would you want to join us?" I asked.

"No," he told me. "I'll stay home. It was too early a flight for me. I need to catch up on sleep," Kevin replied. So, I gave him a kiss and left with James to begin our day.

As we began our ride, I wondered why Kevin would decide to spend two weeks at my place without informing me ahead of time, considering our current tension. I wasn't totally surprised, Kevin had always had a sense of ownership of me throughout our years.

The Peoples' Place, a non-profit organization focused on helping immigrants settle in the United States was the center James and I were looking at volunteering as legal advisers. It was a center that provided various services such as legal advice, housing recommendations, language lessons and much more. The center had immigrants from all over the world and they were opened six days a week. The location was a one-level, red bricked building with a sense of age from the outside. Inside of the building, the walls were painted grey and little dividers separated the large hall into smaller rooms. As we walked in, there were about fifty people sitting and waiting for services.

They looked scared, unsure and nervous about the future in a strange land. It reminded me of the journey and struggles I and some of my friends had encountered. Despite their worried faces, I was also relieved because I could not wait to experience their success stories years down the road. At the door, we were greeted by a lady who was the director. She and two other staffs were paid while the other eighteen were volunteers. She took us to a section in the room where we discussed in what capacity we would be able to serve. James and I had decided to volunteer on Wednesday and Friday evenings which were non court days for us and we were willing to serve wherever our services were needed.

James dropped me back home after a fulfilling day at the The People's Place. We were thrilled to start our journey as volunteers and to be mentors, especially to the younger generation at the center. The two hours spent at the center were worth it.

I was off work till the following Monday, so I was not going to see James again till next week at work. I didn't have to knock because Kevin saw me through the window as James dropped me off. As I got in, I realized Kevin had been cleaning the living room. He loved cleaning, but I enjoyed cooking and cleaning, so he rarely got the opportunity. I needed to sleep more, my body seemed to have not recovered from the jet lag.

I slept for six hours that afternoon and still woke up feeling very tired. As I made my way to the living room, I could hear th noises of pans and pots as well as a beautiful smell. It smelled like grilled chicken with some extra pepper. Kevin enjoyed extra spicy foods and every time he cooked, I needed enough water to cool down how spicy the dishes were.

Yes, I was right, it was grilled chicken and Dodo with pepper sauce. I didn't expect otherwise because he was good with grilled and fried foods. Kevin had a special touch with his grilled chicken. He used lemon spices and the flavor was irresistible. I could not wait to dive into dinner.

Throughout dinner, I discussed my trip to Cameroon with Kevin. I told him about the difference in infrastructure, more people being educated as well as the shock I got from how open society had become. Kevin had not visited Cameroon since he was eighteen years and he seemed to have lost interest in visiting. We had planned to take a trip together after the wedding so he could meet my siblings and get to spend some time in Cameroon. I told him about the laughter party we had at my mother's grave. My nieces and nephews were all grown and the oldest amongst them was in secondary school getting ready for high school in two years. I wondered how it all happened so fast, I was excited about what the future had in store for my family.

"Babe, I'm happy to see you happy again," Kevin said.

"Yes, its been a horrible past couple of years," I said as I hit my empty plate with my fork.

"When do you want us to have the wedding? I was thinking next year?" Kevin asked.

I stuttered as I looked for words to explain that I was not ready for marriage.

"I think we need more time. I am not sure I want to get ready right now," I said.

"How so? You were the one who wanted to get married before thirty. You are twenty-nine," he said.

"I know, but something different seems to be burning in me right now. A greater perspective and less pressure on being perfect."

"Interesting…Okay. I said I was sorry. Can we let this child thing go away, it's not a big deal." He stood up and walked to the couch.

"Kev, I am certain that I do not want to commit at this moment. I am certain it is not about you having a child. It's more about me figuring out truthfully what I need." I walked closer to him as I said these words. His face was beginning to look darken and he barely drank from his glass of wine since he sat on the couch.

"What's going on? Is it James? For some reason, your relationship with him gets weirder by the day."

My heart skipped when he mentioned James. Did he know about James and me? The nights I'd spent at his place?

"Nothing to do with James. It's just what I need right now, Kev."

"I will give you some space. If you need me, you know where to find me. I cannot do this anymore. It is hurting me." His long fingers began to shake on his glass as he struggled to walk his way to the kitchen "I am out of here," he continued.

My heart kept beating faster. A relationship I had invested so much into seemed to be crumbling. The thunderstorms outside seemed to fill my chest and the heavy rains were not soothing to me for a good night rest as they would normally. Memories of Kevin flashed through my head, the good, bad and unique experiences cluttered my brain at that moment.

Ngang, when translated in my language, means salt. The very essence of life is when we can begin to add value to the lives of others. The words of my elder brother could not be any more handy at this moment. He said, "Sis, no matter how many rooms you have in a house, you can only sleep in one."

These words began to redefine my purpose. The definition of success could not be limited to the material world of success, which for me was represented by Kevin. Something in this moment made me bolder. I felt there were more people in the room than myself. I finally had the courage to be free from expectations. I was sweating profusely in my sweatpants and sweatshirt even though it was a cold evening. The thunderstorms and heavy rains ironically provided me with the illusion of approval. That my next actions were approved in heaven by sending down the rain. I picked up my purse from the chair, pulled on jacket, and ran out of the building. My heart knew what I wanted. As I embarked on my twenty minute drive , memories with James filled the moments. The lunch breaks we took together, the dinner dates with our partners, visiting each other. I had no pressures to be perfect with him.

His dance moves were worse than mine, yet that made me want to dance with him all the more. The ride could not be any longer, I sure was not alone in the car. I could feel my parents and Ms. Smith in the car cheering me on for finally letting go of the burden I had placed on myself under.

I arrived at my destination and under the heavy rain I ran to the door, drops of water dripping from my wet braids. Yet I wasn't concerned about the hours I had spent to get the braids done., I had to do this.I knocked very strongly at the door with my both hands until the owner opened the door. There was James even though he was shocked to see me, he opened his arms to give me a hug. I had grown to love this man, his humility and friendship had touched my heart and I could no longer fight my feelings. As we kissed glued in each other's arms my wet clothes seemed not to have bother him . I had no worries about the future. I was confident, it would be *fine* with James.

www.ingramcontent.com/pod-product-compliance
Lightning Source LLC
Chambersburg PA
CBHW070829250626
47170CB00006B/2262